HAYLEY the Hairy Horse

Gavin Puckett

Illustrated by Tor Freeman

90 YEARS OF EXCELLENCE

FABER & FABER

Hello, young reader . . . !

Thanks for taking the time,
In selecting my book of ridiculous rhyme.
I'm Gavin (you'll find my full name on
        the cover),
The teller of tales, which you're soon to
        discover.
It's taken me years to unearth these
        strange fables,
By visiting farmyards and hanging round
        stables,

And this is a series with just a selection
Of some of the weirdest in my
        collection.
They're all about horses –
        each one of them true –
And it's such a nice privilege to share
        them with you!
Well, when I say *"True,"* I mean . . .
        that's what I've heard.
(It's hard to believe, since they're all so
        absurd!)
So, instead of returning this book to the
        shelf,
Why not read on and decide for yourself?

At the edge of a town, on a

large patch of land,

I know of a factory, *majestic* and *grand*.

It has dozens of horses who work there

each day,

Merrily toiling away for their pay.

But what do they do there . . . ?

What is their task . . . ?

These are logical questions

you're sure to ask.

Well . . . each lovely horse is
        providing a trade,
By supplying its hair so that
        stuff can be made.
Bristles for paintbrushes,
        stuffing for seats,
Even wall insulation
        to keep in the heat.
And the hair from their tails
        (as I'm sure you all know)

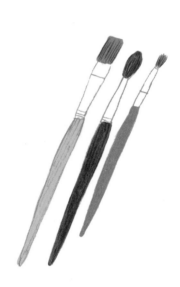

Is *essential* for instruments played
with a bow.
A role is assigned to each
animal there,
Depending of course on the
style of their hair.

Insulation and stuffing requires a horse
Whose coat is quite shaggy –
or bushy and
coarse.

Brushes for painting need hair

sharp and fine.

Whereas *musical* bows require strong

strands like twine.

When a horse isn't filling its face

from a trough,

It works three days a week and

has fourteen days off.

They're groomed, they're all pampered,

and each free to roam

Through the acres of green fields

surrounding their home.

Hayley the horse was considered *the best*,

As her hair was quite special

compared to the rest.

Her sleek tail was glossy,

her black mane *perfection*.

Her coat shone so bright you could

see your reflection.

They took Hayley's locks

to make quality things,

Like the paintbrushes used to craft

portraits of kings,

Or the bows made for violins played

by musicians,

Performing all Beethoven's

    fine compositions.

The factory owner was Mr Maclean.

He was such a nice chap,

    and not at all mean.

This kind and considerate, jolly old soul

Had taken in Hayley when she was a foal.

He raised her and cared for her

    (just like the others),

And brought them together like

    sisters and brothers.

But Hayley, in time,

    had become rather jaded,

Her love for the factory

    had gradually faded.

She grew tired of the horses
and Mr Maclean,
And was bored by the tedious
daily routine.
Don't get me wrong, Hayley's
job wasn't tough.
I suppose you could say
it just wasn't enough.

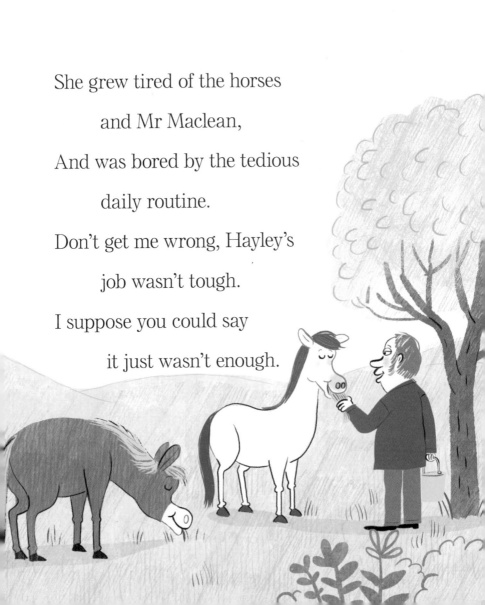

One day at the factory,

Mr Maclean

Had a phone call from

someone who

worked for the queen.

'It's Her Majesty's birthday,'

the caller explained.

'And we need your help keeping

our guests entertained.'

The man told Maclean

that the whole of the nation

Was eager to watch

this unique celebration,

As a famous violinist called

Vincent La Rue

Would be playing onstage

with his orchestra too.

The man also explained that

before every show,

La Rue tied new hair to

his violin bow.

(Apparently *Vincent La Rue*

 always found

That freshly cut strands gave

 a much better sound.)

But there wasn't much time –

 the schedule was tight –

As the concert was planned for the

 following night.

'Could La Rue try some samples?' the man

 asked Maclean.

'Only the best hair will do

for our queen!'

With a feeling of *honour*,

Maclean said,

'Of course!

Send him tomorrow . . .

I have just the

horse!'

The following day,

   around twenty past four,

Maclean heard a knock on

   the factory door.

When he answered, a man uttered,

   'How do you do?'

(In a very posh voice . . .)

   It was *Vincent La Rue.*

La Rue was quite **tall**

   and was *painfully* thin,

16

With a long pointy nose

and a *sticky-out* chin.

He had gangly fingers

and neatly cut nails,

And was wearing a black velvet jacket

with tails.

The man had a walk that was

springy and **bouncy**,

And silvery hair which was

floppy and **flouncy**.

'Show me the hair!'

the musician

commanded.

'I don't have all day. Hurry up!'

he demanded.

Maclean gave a nod,

without any

debating,

And informed the musician

he had a horse waiting.

La Rue pushed his way

    through a large wooden door

To a room at the back

    of the factory floor.

When he first spotted Hayley,

    he halted his stride,

His bottom jaw dropped,

    and his eyes opened wide.

Lost in the moment,

    La Rue couldn't speak,

As he pressed Hayley's tail

to the side of his cheek.

It was soft, smooth and silky,

yet **STRONG** as can be.

'Astonishing . . . ! Stunning!'

he spluttered with glee.

Vincent yelled out

(with one final inspection . . .),

'I'll take her whole tail!

This hair is *perfection*!'

Poor Hayley trembled,

her heart sk^{i}pped a beat,

She whinnied and neighed,

and she shuffled her feet.

She was used to them taking

the odd strand or two –

Not the whole bloomin' thing . . . !

What was she to do?

But Maclean eased her fears

with a shake of his head.

'I'm sorry, you can't have

it all!' the man said.

La Rue was **aghast** –

 he demanded and pleaded –

Claiming **that tail**

 was the one thing he needed.

For hair such as this –

 hair so *silken*, yet **tough** –

Was a rare thing to find,

 there just wasn't enough.

Still . . . the answer was, 'No!'

 and Maclean stood his ground,

Before offering Vincent,

'Five strands for a pound.'

'That simply won't do!'

said La Rue with a tut,

And he bounded away

with an *arrogant* **strut**.

The musician passed Hayley

and bid her goodbye

With a piercing mischievous

glint in his eye.

For La Rue had a plan

    (the despicable creep)

To steal Hayley's tail

    when the horse was asleep!

Later that day,

    with the factory closed,

As the horses lay down in their quarters

    and dozed,

La Rue climbed the fence,

    feeling ready and able,

And silently tiptoed

towards Hayley's stable.

With a spring in his step

and his cutters in hand,

La Rue pushed her door

as he'd deviously planned.

Hayley awoke with a startled

surprise,

And looked back at the man

through her sleep-ridden

eyes.

When she saw who it was,

she felt *flutters* inside.

She leaped to her feet and her stance

became w i d e.

Hayley had to be **strong** –

this horse couldn't fail –

There was no way on earth

he was taking her tail!

La Rue snatched her tail,

and he pulled at some strands,

With a hefty old *yank*,

using one of his

hands.

Hayley's face

grimaced,

she clenched her

teeth tight,

Before clamping her

bum cheeks with

all of her might.

La Rue yanked and hauled,

and turned red in the face,

But the tail remained firm,

and stayed stuck to the base.

Hayley by now had had

    more than enough,

And she knew in her mind

    that she had to get **tough**.

She poked out her tongue,

    blew a **raspberry** and neighed,

        Then sat on her tail,

        and that's how

           she stayed.

La Rue tried to move her,

he pushed and he

wriggled.

He tickled her, shook

her, and

joggled

and jiggled.

But despite his best efforts,

this horse didn't squirm.

Hayley sat rigid,

resilient and firm.

The musician was edgy,

    he started to panic,

His mind was a muddle,

    his nerves were now manic.

His concert was only

    an hour away,

And without Hayley's tail,

    La Rue couldn't play.

That's when the man

    had a brilliant idea,

And jumped in the seat of a forklift

parked near.

He sc^{oo}ped up the horse

     with conviction and haste,

And drove through the gate

     leaving no time to waste.

'If I can't chop the tail from

     your body . . .' he said.

'Then I'll just take the rest of you

     with me instead!'

He arrived at the concert

with minutes to spare,

And was met with a sea

of inquisitive glares.

'What's La Rue up to?'

'Where has he been?'

'He's on in two minutes

to play for the queen.'

La Rue felt his whole body

shudder with *rage*,

As he lowered the horse

to the side of the stage.

Hayley just smiled

    and winked back at the man.

Hayley, it seemed,

    had her own cunning plan!

With no spare equipment,

    no alternative aid

(Just his old, precious bow

    and the fiddle he played),

La Rue knew his options

    were nearly depleted,

But **NO WAY** would the **desperate** man

   be defeated!

He had one final chance to

   take part in that show,

So he tied Hayley's tail

   to his violin bow!

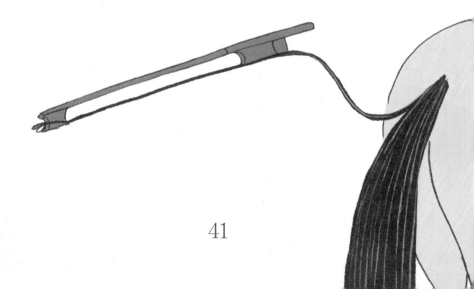

Hayley stood up

    with a grin on her face,

And she held her head high

    with *refinement* and *grace*.

She trotted onstage

    with a satisfied mind,

Now in total control

    of what followed behind.

As the horse gave a curtsey,

    the queen seemed perplexed,

Uncertain of what was about

to come next.

La Rue took a gulp

feeling rather *precarious* . . .

Then lowered the bow

to his old Stradivarius.

When Hayley's tail touched

the first violin string,

It sounded like angels

had started to sing.

There was silence and

    after a (very brief) pause,

The audience cheered

    and began their applause.

La Rue kept on playing,

    all *snooty* and *formal*,

And acted like things

were entirely normal.

His orchestra shrugged,

unsure quite what to do,

And (feeling bewildered)

they played along too.

It didn't take long for

the audience to find

That Hayley had

other ideas on her mind.

She glanced at the crowd

with a mischievous smirk,

Before flicking her tail

with a *delicate* **jerk**.

The bow juddered sharply –

the strings **scratched**

and **jangled** –

Creating a noise

like a cat being strangled.

Hayley kept twitching,

　　La Rue tried resisting,

But each time he fought her,

　　his bow kept on twisting.

The **screeching** was awful

　　and brought with it jeers,

As the audience grimaced

and covered their ears.

La Rue closed his eyes

and he started to curse,

Unaware that things

were about to get worse!

The orchestra winced

(as did **Her Majesty**)

Truly appalled

at this musical travesty.

Hayley kept smiling

   and turned to the crowd,

She glanced at the queen and

   she once again bowed.

Feeling quite cautious,

   with fiddle in hand,

La Rue tried to play

   with the rest of his band.

But as the musician

   was finding his groove,

He realised Hayley

was starting to move.

The horse started walking –

quite slowly at first –

But soon began *trotting*,

and then with a **burst**,

Hayley *leaped* and she *lunged*

with an elegant pr^{an}ce,

She *frolicked* and *shuffled*

and started to da$_n$ce.

La Rue could now tell

    he was destined to fail,

So he grappled the bow

    that was tied to her tail.

He screamed with anxiety,

'Get me a knife!'

Afraid to let go, he hung on

for his life!

Hayley kept *dancing* and *prancing*

and *swirling* . . .

And, with Vincent attached,

the horse started *twirling*.

Vincent La Rue felt his
feet leave the ground,
And got dizzy as Hayley
began to spin round.

In seconds, the man

    was a **spiralling blur**.

'Stop . . . I feel sick!'

    he cried out with a slur.

With one final spin

    that was hefty and slick,

The horse gave her tail

    a remarkable flick.

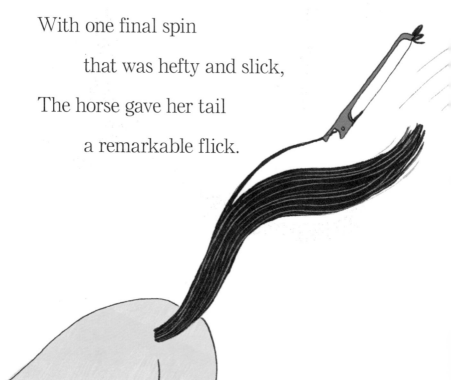

The queen gasped aloud,

in a state of despair,

As she watched the man *fly*

like a bird through the air.

He fell to the ground
with a **crash** and a **bump**,
And remained on the floor
in a wobbly slump.
The audience *groaned*
and they silently gazed
At the horse on the stage,
feeling baffled and dazed.
Then **Her Majesty** spoke
on behalf of the nation:

'I do hope that one

  has a good explanation!'

With a nod of her head,

  Hayley spoke to **the queen**,

And informed her she worked

  for a man called Maclean.

When she mentioned La Rue

  had tried stealing her tail,

Her Majesty's face

  turned a *grey shade* of pale.

The musician stayed silent

with guilt on his face,

And **gawked** at **the queen**,

full of shame and disgrace.

The crowd started booing and

then (with a wail)

A man yelled, '**Your Majesty** . . .

sling him in jail!'

But **the queen** simply smiled

and held up her arm,

Requesting the crowd

to stay silent and calm.

She called Hayley close

and she spoke in her ear.

When she'd finished, she asked,

'Can you do that, my dear?'

Hayley just chuckled

and told her she could.

Her Majesty winked at the horse

and said, 'Good!'

Hayley leaned down

towards *Vincent La Rue*,

Just like the queen

had instructed her to.

His flouncy grey hair

was a **terrible mess**,

And he slouched on the ground

with a look of distress.

When she clamped her teeth down

on his silvery mop,

La Rue started begging for

Hayley to stop.

'Let's see how you like it!'

Her Majesty said,

As the horse snatched the wig

from the top of his head.

The crowd started laughing

(the orchestra too),

As they pointed and sniggered

at *Vincent La Rue*.

'He's wearing a wig!'

they bellowed and called . . .

'Look at La Rue . . .

     the man is quite bald!'

The musician leaped to his feet

     in a **rage**,

And clutching his head

     he bounded offstage.

The queen patted Hayley

     and pulled the horse near,

And she said with a smile,

     'Come and live with me, dear.'

Hayley's face beamed.

  She leaped up and pranced.

'Yes please!' cried the horse,

  as she once again danced.

But then Hayley turned and saw

Mr Maclean,

Who clambered onstage,

stopping next to **the queen**.

'Thank goodness you're safe!

I'm so glad you're all right.

From now on, I won't let you

out of my sight.'

He kissed Hayley's nose

and he cradled her face,

Before hugging her neck

with a *loving* embrace.

Then he gazed at his horse

with a deep sense of pride,

Which gave her

a *warm fuzzy* feeling inside.

As the horse peered back

towards Mr Maclean,

She pictured her stable –

the acres of **green** –

She felt the man's **love** and

affection shine through,

And at that very moment,

the horse felt love too.

That's when she realised

that actually

68

There was only one place

she wanted to be.

The place where her friends were,

  where horses could roam,

The **wonderful** factory,

  the place she called **home!**

So off they both went

to that large patch of land,

Back to the factory,

majestic and *grand*.

Though things for this filly

were never the same –

Not after Hayley

had risen to fame.

You see, Hayley still lives there

with Mr Maclean,

But once every fortnight

she visits **the queen**.

Her Majesty loves her,

and often requests

For the horse to take stage

and perform for her guests.

So Hayley now offers

the *royal musicians*